THE PURIM GOAT

CHILDREN'S BOOKS BY YURI SUHL

Simon Boom Gives a Wedding
The Man Who Made Everyone Late
Simon Boom Gets a Letter
The Merrymaker
Eloquent Crusader: Ernestine Rose (A Biography)
An Album of the Jews in America (A Pictorial History)
Uncle Misha's Partisans (A Novel)
On the Other Side of the Gate (A Novel)

THE PURIM GOAT

by YURI SUHL

illustrated by KAETHE ZEMACH

FOUR WINDS PRESS   NEW YORK

To Isabelle

LIBRARY OF CONGRESS CATALOGING IN PUBLICATION DATA

Suhl, Yuri
    The Purim goat.

    Summary: Hoping to earn some money so his pet goat
won't be sold to pay a debt, a poor Jewish boy teaches the
animal to dance.
    [1. Jews in Eastern Europe—Fiction.   2. Goats—Fiction.
    3. Poverty—Fiction]   I. Zemach, Kaethe.   II. Title.
PZ7.S9445Pu   [Fic]
                  ISBN 0-590-07658-2

PUBLISHED BY FOUR WINDS PRESS
A DIVISION OF SCHOLASTIC MAGAZINES, INC., NEW YORK, N.Y.
TEXT COPYRIGHT © 1980 BY YURI SUHL
ILLUSTRATIONS COPYRIGHT © 1980 BY KAETHE ZEMACH
ALL RIGHTS RESERVED
PRINTED IN THE UNITED STATES OF AMERICA
LIBRARY OF CONGRESS CATALOG CARD NUMBER: 79-6551
            1   2   3   4   5   84   83   82   81   80

In the small town of Betchootch—a name that sounds like a sneeze—where the houses were made of clay and the roofs were thatched, and the mud never dried on the unpaved streets, there once lived a poor widow named Braindel with her son, Yossele, who was ten years old.

In Betchootch, where the rich were few and the poor were many, Braindel seemed the poorest of all. Her small clay house had only one room, which was sparsely furnished—two low wooden beds, two old rickety chairs that creaked when you sat on them, and a square, wooden table whose legs were never steady because the earthen floor on which they stood was bumpy and uneven.

Braindel supported herself and her son by selling roasted pumpkin seeds on the town square for a groshen a measure. She didn't earn much even on sunny days when people liked to go promenading on the square; on rainy days, when the square was almost empty, Braindel and Yossele frequently went to bed hungry.

Her best day was Thursday, which was fair day in Betchootch. On that day the peasants came in from the country to trade with the townspeople. They brought basketsful of fresh fruit and vegetables, fresh eggs and freshly churned butter, and live chickens to sell to the housewives, and sometimes calves and goats to sell to the butcher.

With the money from their sales the peasants bought from the town's merchants things they displayed in their stalls, such as yard goods and dry goods, shoes and boots, hats and caps, kitchenware and earthenware, tin pails and wooden troughs, ribbons, buckles and belts, twine and shoelaces, thimbles, needles and thread. There was a saying in Betchootch: "If you do well on fair day, you eat well the rest of the week."

On the day of the fair Yossele did not go to cheder. Instead he went with his mother to the square to help her sell pumpkin seeds. Their favorite spot was next to the blind organ-grinder whose green-feathered parrot, Katya, always drew a large crowd. Katya could whistle, imitate voices, and cry out: "Hello everybody! Hello everybody!"

Braindel would sit on a low stool with her merchandise on her lap and Yossele would call out in his young, strong voice: "Pumpkin seeds. Get your fresh-roasted pumpkin seeds. One groshen a measure."

After hearing Yossele's call a few times the parrot would imitate him and cry out in her thick, gurgling voice: "Pumpkin seeds. Pumpkin seeds!" When that happened the crowd roared with laughter and the sale of pumpkin seeds went up.

But selling pumpkin seeds was only a groshen business and even with the aid of Katya, the parrot, Braindel's earnings were not enough to make ends meet.

One day Braindel heard that Reb Todres, the sugar merchant, needed a quart of fresh goat's milk every day for his ailing son, Velvele; and because no one in Betchootch owned a goat that gave milk he had to send his coachman every day to a farm to buy it.

So Braindel went to Reb Todres, who lived in a big house in the better section of town, and asked him if he would be willing to buy the milk from her.

"Certainly," said Reb Todres. "Why not? It'll save me the trouble of sending my coachman every day to a farm. When can you start delivering?"

"As soon as I get a goat," Braindel told him.

"And when will that be?"

"As soon as I get the money to buy the goat."

"And when will *that* be?" Reb Todres wanted to know.

"That's up to you, Reb Todres," Braindel said. "If you'll lend me ten rubles it could happen even tomorrow."

"That *would* be soon," said Reb Todres, and he wrapped his hand around his long, red beard and squeezed it hard while he made up his mind. "All right," he finally announced. "I'll lend you the rubles and you'll pay them back to me in milk."

"We are lucky, my son," Braindel announced, waving the ten rubles in her hand. "With God's help we will soon have a goat. Now let's go to bed. Tomorrow is fair day and we must rise very early, earlier than usual."

"Why earlier than usual, Mother?"

"So we can be there before the goats are sold to the butcher."

Long after Braindel had turned out the kerosene lamp Yossele was still awake, thinking about the goat. "Mother," he called out to her in the dark.

"Yes, my son."

"Where will the goat sleep?"

"Under the bed, I suppose. There's hardly any room elsewhere."

"Under your bed, or mine?"

"You want her to sleep under your bed? You can have the pleasure."

"Mother?"

"Yes?"

"What will we feed the goat?"

"I don't know. I never had a goat to supper. We'll ask the peasant who'll sell us the goat."

"Mother?"

"What now?"

"Do goats eat pumpkin seeds?"

"I hope not. And if they do this one won't. Now go to sleep, Yossele; enough questions for one night."

But long after Yossele had fallen asleep Braindel was still awake, thinking about all the things she would do after she had paid off her debt to Reb Todres: Yossele's shoes needed soling, and there were more patches on his trousers than she could count. She'd take him first to the tailor and have him measured for a new suit, and after that was paid off she'd take him to the cobbler. As for herself, she'd settle for a decent dress for the

Sabbath. And she'd pay off all the old debts to the grocer and the butcher so her credit would be good again. And, of course, she'd be able to afford a piece of meat from time to time, and a piece of chicken for the Sabbath meal. The thoughts that kept her awake were so pleasant she didn't mind not falling asleep.

The next morning mother and son were up early and, after their usual breakfast of chicory and black bread, they hurried to the fair to look for a goat. They found only one goat for sale, a frail, skinny-looking animal that Reb Beinish, the butcher, had already seen and passed up.

"How much do you want for her?" Braindel asked.

"Thirteen rubles," said the peasant.

"For this cadaver of a goat you ask thirteen rubles?"

"All right," said the peasant. "Give me twelve and you have yourself a bargain."

"For this skeleton of a goat you want twelve rubles?"

"All right, give eleven and it's a deal."

In the meantime Yossele was busy making friends with the goat. He patted her bony body, played with her short tail and touched the tips of her tiny horns. The goat was so pleased with

the boy's attention that she looked at him gratefully with her large, brown eyes and kept butting him gently with her head, as if to say: "More, more."

"What do you say, Yossele," Braindel turned to her son, "shall I buy her?"

"Buy her, Mother, buy her," Yossele urged, putting his arm around the goat's scrawny neck and holding her close to him.

"But she's so skinny, her ribs are showing," Braindel said, examining the goat for the tenth time.

"We'll fatten her up, Mother."

"With what, with my troubles?"

"With grass," the peasant chimed in, "and hay, and rolled oats and cracked corn, and some salt water."

"Salt water I can give her plenty," said Braindel, "but where will I get the rest of the things? Betchootch has mud, not grass."

"Tell you what I'll do," said the peasant, slapping his hands together. "Give me eleven rubles and I'll throw in a sack of hay for good measure. Is it a deal?"

"How can I give you eleven rubles when all I have is ten?" said Braindel.

"It's a deal," said the peasant, and untied the goat.

Yossele led the goat home and Braindel, walking beside him, carried the sack of hay.

Now Braindel's one room looked even more crowded than before.

"I already have a place for the goat, Mother," Yossele announced cheerfully.

Braindel looked up and saw the goat standing in a corner near Yossele's bed, looking bewildered and confused. The only indoor place the goat had been to was the peasant's huge barn where she spent the night together with other animals. There was nothing familiar to her in this small room, crowded with strange objects.

"Very good, my son." Braindel was pleased. "Now put some food down for her and tie her to the bedpost; we must hurry back to the fair."

Yossele put down a little heap of hay and a bowl of salted water for the goat but he couldn't bring himself to tie her to the bed.

"You forgot something, Yossele," his mother said, just as they were about to leave the house. "You didn't tie up the goat."

"Must I, Mother?" Yossele said. "It'll make her so unhappy."

"Nonsense, my son. A goat doesn't know from happy or unhappy; she's an animal."

"But she's so perfectly still," Yossele pleaded.

"Right now she is still, but as soon as we leave she'll turn the room upside down. Go, Yossele, do as I tell you."

Reluctantly Yossele walked over to the goat. He took the rope that hung from her neck into his right hand and with his left he patted her back. The goat butted him gently with her head as she had done earlier on the square when he played with her. But a moment later the goat sensed that this was no game. As soon as she felt herself tied to the bed she pulled at the rope, jerking her head forward and sideways struggling to free herself. Yossele tried to soothe her by patting her again but the goat ignored him as though he were a stranger and continued pulling at the rope.

"She doesn't want to be tied up, Mother," Yossele cried, his eyes brimming with tears. "Can't you see?"

"She'll get used to it, my son," Braindel said. "Come, come. Once we're out of the house she'll settle down."

All the way to the fair Yossele walked in sullen silence. He felt guilty for what he had done to the goat. If he could only tell her in plain words that he trusted her, that it was not *his* idea to tie her up but that he was merely obeying his mother. If he could somehow make her understand that, he thought, the goat might forgive him. But how? He could think of only one way—by not doing it again. The next time his mother would ask him to tie up the goat he would tell her she would have to do it herself. But wouldn't it be a sin not to obey his mother?

"Hello everybody! Hello everybody!" The parrot's screeching voice broke into his thoughts, reminding him that they were already at the fair.

All of Betchootch seemed to have crowded into the square. Sellers were hawking their wares; people were clustering around stalls; buyers were haggling for bargains. And mixed with the din and noise of the fair were the sad, plaintive melodies of the blind organ-grinder and the high-pitched, raucous greeting of his parrot, Katya: "Hello everybody! Hello everybody!"

"We're late," Braindel muttered unhappily as she and Yossele pushed their way through the jostling crowd. Fortunately, no one had taken her place and all that Braindel had to do was to set herself down on her low stool, put her bag of pumpkin seeds on her lap and she was in business. Yossele, for his part, filled a measureful of seeds and began to circulate around the crowd that the parrot attracted, calling: "Fresh-roasted pumpkin seeds!"

Around noon, when Yossele announced that he was hungry, Braindel gave him a thick slice of black bread. She had baked the bread several days ago and it was still quite fresh and tasty. Then she gave him a groshen and told him to buy himself a pear or an apple from one of the peasants at the fair.

It was the same lunch his mother gave him every morning to

take with him to cheder. Sometimes a raw carrot took the place of the apple or pear, and there were days when there was no carrot either. The only thing he had plenty of was pumpkin seeds. It was a lucky day when a cheder-mate was willing to barter a piece of buttered bread for a handful of seeds.

"Mother?"

"Yes, my son."

"Can you make butter from goat's milk?"

"I've heard of goat's cheese, but not of goat's butter."

"Will you milk her today?"

"As soon as we get home from the fair."

"Will I take the milk to Reb Todres?"

"If there'll be anything to take you will. First let me see what that skinny bargain of mine can give. If she'll give a full quart you'll take it to Reb Todres."

"She will, Mother, she will. You wait and see."

"I hope you are right, my son," Braindel sighed. "You have more faith in her than I."

Late in the afternoon the crowds began to dwindle and the fair was winding down. Peasants who had sold their produce were hurrying back to their farms; merchants were calling out their last-minute bargains as they were gathering in their wares; the organ-grinder's parrot was still screaming, "Hello everybody!" but hardly anyone listened. Everybody was eager to get home before sundown; and Yossele, it seemed, was more eager than anybody else. He wanted to get home as quickly as possible and untie the goat from the bedpost.

But when Yossele and his mother came into the house there was no goat to untie. All that was still tied to the bedpost was a piece of rope. The goat was nowhere in sight. And when Braindel looked around the room she let out a gasp. The chairs were knocked over, the curtains pulled down, the bedspreads messed up and, worst of all, the sack of pumpkin seeds which stood near the stove was ripped open and the seeds were scattered on the floor.

"Woe is me!" Braindel wrung her hands in despair. "It looks like after a hurricane."

"She's gone, Mother!" Yossele cried. "The goat is gone!"

"Our livelihood is spilled on the floor and you worry about the goat. Did you look under the beds?"

"I did, Mother, I already did," he said, bursting into tears. "She ran away."

"How could she have run away when the window is closed and the door was locked? She's still in the room somewhere and we'll find her. But first let's pick up the seeds from the floor before we trample on our only piece of bread."

They both got down on their knees and began picking up the scattered pumpkin seeds. They were almost finished when they heard a faint baaing.

"She's here!" Yossele cried jubilantly and sprang to his feet. "Where are you, goat?" he called out, looking around the room.

"Baa, baa," came the goat's weak reply.

"It's her voice, all right," Yossele said, "but where is she?"

Now Braindel, too, was on her feet. "Where are you, my skinny bargain?" she called. "I bought a goat, not a ghost."

They both held their breath, straining for the goat's voice. After a long silence it came, this time louder than before. "I think it came from there," Yossele said, pointing to the oven.

He was right. The goat had somehow managed to scramble up into the oven, and now she didn't know how to get out. The oven was too narrow for her to turn around.

"Hand me the broom, Yossele," Braindel said.

"What will you do, Mother?"

"Give her a few pokes with the broomstick so she'll come out."

"No, Mother, you'll hurt her. I'll get her out." He used his mother's low stool to get himself up a little higher. Then he put his hands deep into the oven and reached for the goat's hind legs. Slowly and carefully he began pulling her toward him.

"Backward, backward," Yossele talked to the goat, "move backward."

The goat seemed to understand. And as soon as her rump came close to the edge they both pulled her out of the oven and set her down on the floor. The goat stared at them with her brown eyes and let out a loud "baa-aa;" then she turned to Yossele and butted him with her head.

"She's not mad at me, Mother," Yossele said, smiling. "She butted me."

"Why should *she* be mad at *you*?"

"For having tied her up."

"Well, I am plenty mad with her for doing what she did. Now take her out for a while so I can open the window to air out the room, and straighten up this mess."

Braindel had never milked a goat before. But she remembered that as a little girl she was once taken to a farm and there watched a farm maid milk a cow. The maid, seated on a low stool, had pulled at the cow's teats with both hands and milk came squirting into a pail in rapid streams, making a swishing sound: swish-swish, swish-swish.

Now Braindel did the same with the goat but the results were different. Instead of rapid streams there were wavering trickles; and instead of swish-swish, swish-swish there was drip-drip, drip-drip. And soon there wasn't even that.

"Woe is me," Braindel cried when she measured the amount of milk. "It's barely half a quart, and Reb Todres needs a full quart."

"Maybe it's because she lost her appetite," Yossele came to the goat's defense. "She didn't touch the hay I left her."

"What did she need hay for when she gorged herself on pumpkin seeds?" Braindel asked. "Now I'll have another worry

on my head. Where will I hide the bag of pumpkin seeds from her? In the trunk they'll get soggy; in the attic the mice will get them." She decided to put the bag of pumpkin seeds under her pillow.

Just before they went to bed Braindel found a strong rope in the trunk and began to tie the goat to Yossele's bed.

"Why did you tie her up when we are home?" Yossele asked.

"We may be home but we'll be sleeping," Braindel explained, "and I don't want to get up in the morning and find the room a shambles."

"Please, Mother," Yossele begged, "don't tie her up. I promise you, nothing will happen."

"*You* promise me. What makes you so sure?"

"Because she doesn't like being tied up. That's why she broke loose from the rope and did what she did."

"Well, she won't break loose from *this* rope. It's twice as strong as the other."

Yossele did not argue anymore, but when they had gone to bed he deliberately stayed awake till his mother was asleep; then he carefully untied the goat and waited to see what she would do.

Around midnight Yossele heard the goat stir. He watched her rise on her spindly legs and walk quietly to the window. Is she going to tear the curtains down again? he wondered, holding his breath. She stood up on her hind legs and, resting her front legs on the windowsill, she looked out into the street, as though curious to see what muddy Betchootch looked like in the moonlight. Having satisfied her curiosity she returned to the little heap of hay which she had made her bed, next to Yossele's, and dozed off.

Now Yossele knew that he didn't have to stay awake anymore and he fell into a deep, satisfying sleep.

He was always awakened by his mother but this morning it

was the goat who woke him with a few little butts of her head. "Ba-a-a," she greeted him when he opened his eyes.

"Shush," Yossele whispered, "you'll wake up Mother." He got out of bed and dressed hurriedly. "Come," he motioned to the goat, and quietly they left the house together.

Betchootch was slowly coming awake. Here and there smoke was rising from a chimney; a servant girl, draped in a shawl and carrying a small shopping basket, was on her way to the bakery for fresh breakfast rolls; a Jew, wearing a long black caftan, was hurrying to the synagogue for early services; and Reb Feivish the water carrier, a short, squat man with broad shoulders and a large beard the color of rust, was making his first delivery.

The unfamiliar sight of a boy and a goat coming toward him aroused the water carrier's curiosity. He stopped and, setting down his two full cans, asked Yossele, "Where did you get that skinny runt of a goat?"

Yossele didn't like the way Reb Feivish spoke of his new friend. The goat may have been skinny but in Yossele's eyes she was not a runt. Still he answered politely, "My mother bought her at the fair." And before Reb Feivish managed to ask him another question Yossele and the goat were gone.

Yossele set a brisk pace and the goat kept up with him as they walked side by side through the narrow, half-deserted streets.

Whenever they came upon a mud puddle they both leaped over it together.

They were out about half an hour and when they came home Braindel was already up and breakfast was ready. But before Yossele sat down to eat he first fed the goat. He had taken upon himself the responsibility of caring for the animal. Only the milking he left to his mother.

Before leaving the house Braindel once again asked Yossele to tie the goat to his bed for the day. Yossele refused.

"Then I'll tie her up myself," Braindel said.

As she started for the rope Yossele planted himself between her and the goat. "Please, Mother," he said, "don't tie her up or you'll find the same mess you found yesterday."

"This rope is much thicker than yesterday's," Braindel told him.

"That makes no difference, Mother. Goats can chew through any rope they want to."

"Then how come she didn't chew it through last night?"

"Because she wasn't tied up last night."

"Have you forgotten? I tied her up with my own hands."

"And I untied her with my own hands," Yossele said.

"You did?" Braindel stared at him in disbelief. "Why did you do that?"

"I *had* to do it, Mother. I had to prove to you that you could trust her. It's only when you tie her up like a prisoner that she goes on a rampage."

Braindel thought a moment and said, "All right, my son. This time I'll take your advice. I hope I won't regret it."

Later that day, when Braindel came home from the town square, she found the room exactly as she had left it in the morning. Everything was in its place. Even the bag of pumpkin seeds was still under the pillow untouched. And the goat lay curled up on the floor near Yossele's bed, looking half asleep.

"Today you behaved like a mentsh," Braindel said to the goat. "Now, if you would only behave like a goat and give a quart of milk a day you could be skinny all you want and you'd still be a bargain."

The goat gave no indication that she understood what Braindel said. She didn't even say "Baa."

Braindel put the rope away in the trunk and never took it out again.

In the meantime Reb Feivish, the water carrier, went from house to house to make his deliveries. But it was not only water that he delivered. He had a habit of bringing his customers the latest bits of news and gossip that he'd picked up along the way.

On this day his latest news was that Braindel, the widow, had bought a goat—not an ordinary goat but a skinny runt of a goat.

It was the kind of news that could give a small town like Betchootch much to talk about. In the first place, his customers wondered, what would Braindel, the widow, want with a goat?

And in the second place, they wondered, where did Braindel, the widow, who supported herself from selling pumpkin seeds, get the money to buy a goat?

And there were some who were sure that the water carrier was in error, that it wasn't Braindel the widow who had bought a goat but Reb Beinish the butcher. That made sense.

And there were others to whom it didn't make any sense at all, because, they argued, why would a butcher buy a skinny runt of a goat? What would he get out of her?

The only one who didn't have to wonder and speculate was Reb Todres. As soon as he heard the news about the goat he immediately dispatched one of his servants to Braindel to find out why she hadn't delivered the quart of goat's milk.

The servant brought back the following reply from Braindel: "Right now the goat gives only a half quart of milk. As soon as she will give a full quart I will start delivering." Whereupon Reb Todres sent the servant back with this message: "I can't wait indefinitely. If in a week's time the goat does not give a full quart I would like my money back. Otherwise I will have to take the matter to the rabbi."

The next day when Reb Feivish delivered his two cans of water to Reb Todres's kitchen the servant girl told him word for word what Reb Todres had told her to say to Braindel the day before. The water carrier repeated the story to all his other customers and now Betchootch had something new to talk

about: Will the matter of Braindel's goat come before the rabbi or not?

On this question Betchootch was divided into two camps, one large and the other small. The larger camp held that if the matter did come before the rabbi, he should decide in Braindel's favor. She's a poor widow, they argued, a pauper seven times over, who lives on the meager earnings from her pumpkin seeds. And on rainy days she earns nothing.

Therefore, they concluded, justice demands that Braindel be allowed to keep her goat and that Reb Todres's son be satisfied with a half quart a day. Where is it written that a boy who has everything his heart desires must also have a full quart of goat's milk a day?

The others disagreed. Reb Todres is an honest and pious Jew, they countered. He and Braindel made a business deal. He loaned her the ten rubles on condition that she pay it back to him in goat's milk, a quart a day. He lived up to his promise. She did not live up to hers. It's not his fault that the goat gives only a half quart a day. A deal is a deal. Therefore justice demands that if Braindel can't deliver a quart a day she must either return the money or the goat belongs to Reb Todres.

And while Betchootch was buzzing with talk about a poor widow, a rich sugar merchant and a skinny goat, Braindel and Yossele were hoping for a miracle. But the miracle did not come. Each day, when the milking was over, all there was in the pot was a half quart of milk, not a drop more, not a drop less.

In the meantime the week was coming to an end and the day of the hearing was approaching. And one bright, sunny morning in March, just when Yossele was about to go off to cheder and Braindel to the town square, Reb Feitel, the shamus, arrived. He was a tall, skinny man with a sparse black beard, a high-pitched voice and a large Adam's apple. Whenever he was excited, he spoke with a slight stutter, and on this morning, like everyone else in Betchootch, Reb Feitel was excited. "I am here to tell you," he said to Braindel, "that you must come at once to the rabbi together with the g-g-g-goat."

"I am coming with you, Mother," Yossele announced with determination.

"No, my son," said Braindel. "There's no need for you to miss a day of cheder. If the rabbi wanted you, he would have said so."

"That's right," Reb Feitel added, in his high, squeaky voice. "The rabbi wants to see only your mother and the g-g-g-goat."

The goat lay curled up near Yossele's bed.

"Come, my big bargain," Braindel said, reaching for the rope collar around the goat's neck. The goat didn't budge. She pulled a little harder and still the goat refused to rise. "Maybe she'll have a little more respect for you, Reb Feitel," Braindel said to the shamus.

Reb Feitel drew himself up even taller than he was and, looking straight at the goat, said in a voice even higher and squeakier than usual, "In the name of our esteemed rabbi, Reb Dovidl, I command you to rise at once and come with us."

"She seems to have as much respect for you as she has for me," Braindel sighed. "What shall we do, Reb Feitel?"

"I don't know." Reb Feitel shook his head unhappily. "In all my years as a shamus I never had any dealings with a g-g-g-goat. All I know, Braindel, is that we have to bring her to the rabbi even if we have to carry her there."

"If you want to carry her, Reb Feitel, the pleasure is yours. I won't make myself the laughing stock of Betchootch," Braindel told him.

"I have no other choice," the shamus said. "The rabbi's orders must be obeyed." And having said this he bent down and started lifting up the goat. The goat resisted, kicking him frantically with both her front and hind legs till he let go of her.

"There's only one thing to do," said the shamus, panting for breath from exertion. "I'll have to tie her legs."

"You will *not* tie her legs!" Yossele cried in a voice so loud even the goat was startled. "I won't let you."

"All right, my son," Braindel sighed. "You will take her to the rabbi. With you she'll go."

Yossele went over to the goat and patted her soothingly to calm her down. Then he rose and said quietly, "Come," and the goat sprang to her legs and followed him out of the house.

Dressed in a dark satin coat and wearing a black velvet skullcap, the rabbi paced the floor of his study lost in thought and looking pale and tired from long hours of study and short hours of sleep. He had been up most of the night searching the ancient books of law that in the past had given him guidance for the disputes that the people brought to him for settlement, but nowhere did he find any mention of a goat that refused to give more than a half quart of milk. No wonder that this morning the rabbi was lost in thought more than usual.

Reb Todres was the first to arrive for the hearing and he seemed to be in a great hurry. "I have a lot of important business to attend to," he informed the rabbi when he saw that Braindel wasn't there yet. "I'm expecting a shipment of sugar from Odessa."

"I sent the shamus for them," the rabbi told Reb Todres. "I don't know what's delaying them so long."

"Them?" Reb Todres looked at the rabbi with surprise.

"Braindel and the goat," the rabbi said.

"The goat?" Reb Todres now stared at the rabbi with astonishment.

"Yes," said the rabbi firmly. "Justice demands that all parties to a dispute be present at the hearing."

"But what can the goat do except smell up this room?" Reb Todres asked.

"Better the smell of the goat than the smell of injustice," said the rabbi.

"Forgive me, esteemed rabbi," said Reb Todres, "but I don't see the wisdom of inviting a goat to a hearing, and a skinny runt of a goat at that."

"Have you yourself seen the goat, Reb Todres?" the rabbi inquired.

"No, I haven't," Reb Todres replied.

"Then how do you know she is a skinny runt of a goat?"

"My wife told me."

"And has your wife seen the goat?" the rabbi wanted to know.

"No, she hasn't. The cook told her."

"And has the cook seen the goat?"

"No, she hasn't. Reb Feivish, the water carrier, told her."

"So what you know about the goat, Reb Todres, is hearsay. And what I know so far is also hearsay. A verdict based on hearsay would not be a just verdict. I must examine the evidence myself. As it is written in the holy books—"

And here the rabbi was interrrupted by a loud babble of voices coming from the street. They went to the window to see what happened and they saw an astonishing sight: a young boy was leading a small goat. Behind him walked Braindel and the shamus. And behind them half of Betchootch.

"Have you sent for all of those people?" Reb Todres asked with alarm.

"No, I haven't," the rabbi replied.

"Then why are they coming here?"

"I suppose they are coming to the hearing," said the rabbi, looking rather pleased.

"I think you should send them away. The hearing is none of their business."

"But it is, Reb Todres, it is," the rabbi said calmly. "Justice is everyone's business. As it is written in the holy books—"

And here the rabbi was interrupted again, this time by the shamus who burst into the room with Yossele, the goat, and Braindel following behind him. He wanted to say something but was too excited to speak.

"Calm yourself, Reb Feitel," the rabbi said quietly, "and tell me what happened, what took so long."

"It's the g-g-g-goat, esteemed rabbi, she didn't want to come."

"Yes, esteemed rabbi," Braindel spoke up for the shamus. "The goat wouldn't come with either of us. Only with my son, Yossele. That's why he's not in cheder now."

The rabbi smiled at Yossele. "We owe you a thanks for bringing this important witness to the hearing," he said, pointing to

the goat. "Now you can go to cheder and if the teacher wants to know why you are late tell him you did an errand for the rabbi."

Reluctantly Yossele left the room. The goat tried to follow him but Braindel held her back.

"We are about to begin the hearing," the rabbi announced. "You, Reb Feitel, be so kind and open the window a bit so that the people standing outside can hear us. And you, Reb Todres, the complainant, have the first word."

"Esteemed rabbi," Reb Todres began, "I have some important business to attend to so I shall be very brief. Braindel came to me one day with a proposition. She would supply me with the quart of goat's milk a day which I need for my ailing son, Velvele, if I advanced her the ten rubles with which to buy the goat. I gave her the money, she bought the goat, a week has passed, and I have not received a single quart of milk. Is it my fault that Braindel's goat gives only a half quart a day? That is all I have to say, esteemed rabbi."

"And what have you to say?" The rabbi turned to Braindel.

"What Reb Todres said is very true, esteemed rabbi," Braindel said. "All I wish to add is this: Is it my fault that the goat refuses to give more than a half quart a day?"

The rabbi turned to the goat and said: "If you were blessed with language you would speak for yourself. But the Almighty in his infinite wisdom has seen fit to endow you with four legs instead of two and not a single word of speech. Therefore we who are endowed with two legs instead of four, but with an abundance of speech, will have to speak for you. As it is written in the holy books—" And here the rabbi was interrupted again, this time by the goat.

A fly, it seems, had landed on Braindel's forehead. Without even thinking about it she removed her hand from the goat to brush it off. And in that moment the goat made a dash for the window and leaped out. Before anyone in the room realized what happened the goat was already far away from the rabbi's house with a crowd running after her.

The goat outran her pursuers, leaping swiftly and gracefully over puddles and fences like a young gazelle. She was heading straight for Braindel's house. When she got there she raised herself up on her hind legs and peered into the window. She was looking for Yossele.

Not finding him there, the goat ran from house to house and from street to street, stopping at every window along the way for a quick look inside, and always keeping one step ahead of her pursuers.

She stopped running when she came to the window of the cheder. There she spotted Yossele, sitting at a long table with other children, chanting and swaying. With one strong butt of the head she pushed the window open and leaped into the cheder, and then over the table to the side where Yossele sat.

Pandemonium broke loose in the small crowded room. The pupils jumped to their feet, shouting, "Braindel's goat! Braindel's goat!" The teacher, brandishing his cat-o'-nine-tails, shouted, "Quiet! Quiet! Back to your seats!" And the goat, frightened by the noise and commotion, crawled under the table and huddled close to Yossele's legs.

Suddenly, Reb Feitel, the shamus, burst into the room, all out of breath from running, and demanded, "Where is the g-g-g-goat?"

"Here she is," Yossele called out. "Under the table."

"Take her back to the hearing at once," the shamus commanded in his high-pitched, nervous voice. "The rabbi is waiting for her."

As soon as the goat was back in the room the rabbi said, "Now I am ready to announce my decision."

At this point Reb Todres demanded that the window be closed so the goat couldn't escape again. "I have important business to attend to," he explained. "I don't want to be delayed anymore."

"The window must remain open so that the people outside could hear me," the rabbi said, "but Reb Feitel will stand guard to prevent the goat from leaping out."

"It isn't necessary for Reb Feitel to guard the window," Yossele spoke up for the first time. "The goat won't escape anymore."

"What makes you so sure?" Reb Todres asked.

Yossele thought a moment and said, "I just know she won't." To illustrate he walked the goat over to the open window and left her there while he himself returned to his chair. Instantly the goat went back to her place next to Yossele.

"I think we can begin now," the rabbi said, smiling at Yossele and, raising his voice a little so that the people outside would hear him, the rabbi gave his decision:

"That Reb Todres is entitled to a quart of goat's milk a day, goes without saying.

"That Braindel, if she had it, would give him a quart of goat's milk a day, also goes without saying.

"That Braindel, if she had it, would give him his money back, also goes without saying.

"That the goat, if she had it, would give a quart of milk a day, goes without saying.

"That the goat is giving only a half quart a day, also goes without saying. So we must ask ourselves: Would the goat give more milk if she had more flesh on her bones, or would she still give only a half quart even if she weighed twice her present weight? To render a just verdict we must first know the answer to this question. Therefore I propose:

"That Reb Todres continue to buy his quart a day from the peasant.

"That Braindel continue to use the half quart a day for herself and her son.

"That all the people of Betchootch who can spare a few crumbs from their tables should bring them to Braindel's goat until such time when her bones will be covered with flesh and she will be double her weight.

"If by then the goat will still give only a half quart of milk, Braindel should sell her to Reb Beinish, the butcher, and give Reb Todres back his ten rubles. In this way Reb Todres will not bear the burden of an unpaid loan and Braindel will not bear the burden of an unpaid debt. As it is written in the holy books—" And just then the rabbi was interrupted again, this time by a loud cheer from the people outside. "Our rabbi, Reb Dovidl, has done it again," they congratulated each other. "The decision he rendered is worthy of a King Solomon. It is fair. It is just. It is wise."

Yossele was also happy with the rabbi's decision, but not with all of it. He didn't like the part that mentioned Reb Beinesh, the butcher. The goat would never, never be sold to

Reb Beinesh. Not if he could help it. That was *his* decision. And he wasn't going to mention it to a soul. Only to his best friend, Berele, in whom he always confided his innermost secrets.

Though most of the people of Betchootch had worries of their own, about making ends meet and getting through the week between one fair and the next, they still remembered the rabbi's decision and didn't forget Braindel's goat. No matter how scanty their meals, they managed to save a crust of bread, a few lima beans, a boiled carrot, or some other scrap of food for Braindel's goat.

The most enthusiastic supporters of the goat were the children. They collected every scrap and crumb of food they could find, and even knocked on strangers' doors to beg for Braindel's goat. And the goat was no finicky eater. She ate, with great relish, everything that was put before her and looked for more.

Several weeks had passed since the hearing before the rabbi and nothing had changed. The goat hadn't gained an ounce of weight and continued to give only a half quart of milk a day. Not a drop more, not a drop less.

Braindel was beginning to get worried again. How long will the good people of Betchootch go on feeding the goat if nothing happens? she wondered. And where would she get the money to pay Reb Todres back his ten rubles? And what butcher would buy a goat that was skin and bones?

That last question didn't worry Yossele at all. If anything it made him happy to know that so far the goat was safe from Reb Beinish's hands. But where to get the money to pay back Reb Todres *was* something to worry about. Ten rubles was a fortune. His mother would never make it from selling pumpkin seeds for a groshen a measure. If only *he* could do something to earn some money. Then he would pay Reb Todres back his ten rubles and it wouldn't matter anymore whether the goat gained weight or not, or how much milk she gave, or how long the people would continue saving scraps for her. And the goat would, once and for all, be free from all threat of Beinish, the butcher.

But what could he do, a boy of ten, in Betchootch, when his mother, so much older than he, could do no more than sell pumpkin seeds on the square for a groshen a measure? Some nights he lay awake thinking about these things long after his mother had fallen asleep.

One day there was great excitement at the fair. The famous dancing bear, Eliosha, had come to Betchootch to do his act.

Eliosha had once been the star of the Krakow circus and had performed in the greatest halls all over Europe. But when he grew too old to travel long distances and entertain large crowds together with other animals, he was sold to a retired animal trainer who took Eliosha from one small town to the next, to entertain at fairs. This was the first time he had come to Betchootch.

Katya, the organ-grinder's parrot, kept crying, "Hello everybody! Hello everybody!" but on that day no one paid any attention to her. Everybody was now at another part of the square, waiting for Eliosha to make his appearance. Yossele, who had never seen a performing bear before, was also in the crowd.

At last the trainer, a tall man dressed in a green coat, a red cap and red baggy trousers tucked into black boots, opened the door of a huge cage on wheels and out came Eliosha. He looked very old. His whiskers were gray. His eyes were tearing. His belly was sagging. And there were large bald patches on his shaggy brown coat. He was so heavy he could hardly walk a step.

But when the trainer cracked his whip in the air Eliosha sprang to life. He rose on his hind legs and blinked at the crowd. Then the trainer cracked the whip once more and Eliosha began to dance. Round and round he danced while the

people clapped their hands. And the louder they clapped the faster he danced.

After a while the trainer cracked his whip for the third and last time. Eliosha stopped dancing and took a bow. The audience went wild with cheers and applause and threw coins at Eliosha's feet.

Yossele was so fascinated by what he saw that he almost forgot he was supposed to circulate among the crowd and sell seeds.

After watching Eliosha do his act several more times that day, Yossele had an idea: If you can teach a bear how to dance, why not a goat? He had heard about dancing bears even before Eliosha came to Betchootch but he had never heard about dancing goats. If he succeeded it would be something new, something even sensational. The first dancing goat in the world! He would team up with his friend, Berele, and together they would take the goat to all the fairs of nearby towns and villages. In no time they would have enough money to pay Reb Todres back his ten rubles and the goat would be theirs!

Berele, who was Yossele's age, and the son of a poor shoemaker, was as excited about the idea as Yossele was. Between them they decided on a time and place to train the goat where no one could see them. They would be able to keep their plan a secret until the goat was ready to make her first appearance at a Betchootch fair.

Early the next morning, when his mother was still asleep, Yossele tiptoed out of the house, taking the goat with him. He woke up Berele and together they went to a vacant lot past the public bath, the most deserted spot in Betchootch.

As soon as they got there Yossele made the goat stand up on her hind legs by lifting up her front legs and holding them high. He then told Berele to clap his hands and began to lead the goat round and round in a circle.

At first the goat looked at Yossele with bewilderment. She had never done this before and she didn't know what to make of it. But soon she got into the spirit of the thing and followed him without protest even when he increased the tempo of the dance. After a while it was Yossele who had to stop because he grew dizzy from turning so fast.

Remembering that Eliosha's trainer rewarded the bear with a chunk of meat each time he completed his act, Yossele took a handful of pumpkin seeds from his trousers pocket and fed them to the goat.

After a brief rest they started over again. On the third time around it was Berele who danced with the goat and Yossele who clapped his hands.

This was how it began, and from that day on the two friends came every morning to the same spot with the goat, except on the Sabbath, and when it rained.

The goat was a fast learner. By the end of the first week Yossele was already swinging her around in a circle while holding on to only one of her front legs.

And by the end of the second week when Yossele let go of the other front leg the goat continued to go round and round by herself on her two hind legs until Berele stopped clapping his hands.

Clearly, the goat understood what was expected of her and she associated the beginning of clapping with starting to dance, and the end of clapping with stopping to dance.

There was only one more thing for her to learn—how to rise on her hind legs by herself without Yossele's or Berele's help. That became the most difficult part of the training.

Eliosha, the bear, rose on his hind legs as soon as the trainer cracked his whip. But Yossele would not use a whip even if he had one. There must be a way of making the goat respond to his wish without the threat of a whip. He tried talking to her. "Up-up," he would say, raising his hands to give her a hint, but the goat remained standing on all fours.

He tried clapping his hands, first by himself and then together with Berele, and still the goat wouldn't budge. It was frustrating. If only he could think of the right sign or sound that the goat would understand, Yossele thought. But what?

One day it came to him—not on the vacant lot but in cheder.

"Today I will tell you the story of Purim," the teacher announced to the class, and instantly there were happy smiles on the children's faces. Purim was their favorite holiday. On Purim they were allowed to dress up in long coats and funny hats, and go from house to house to collect Purim treats—delicious three-pointed cakes called homantashen, filled with poppy seeds or plum jam. And some coins. It was a holiday of joy and fun. And although they knew the story by heart they were always glad to hear it again.

"In a far and distant land called Persia," the teacher began, and the pupils repeated after him in chorus, "there once reigned a king whose name was Ahasuerus. And it came to pass that the queen, whose name was Vashti, lost favor in the eyes of Ahasuerus and he took onto himself a new wife, a beautiful Jewish girl named Esther.

"And it came to pass that a wicked man named Haman, who was the king's chief advisor, wanted all the Jews of Persia destroyed and he went to Ahasuerus and got his permission to carry out his evil plan.

"And it came to pass that a man named Mordecai, who was a kin of Queen Esther, got wind of Haman's plan. He went to her and said, 'Our people are in peril. Go to your husband, the king, and plead with him to spare our people and not let Haman carry out his evil plan.'

"And Esther said to her kin, Mordecai, 'I cannot go because it is forbidden, even for the queen, to enter the king's chamber without his permission.'

"'But for your people's sake you must go at once even at the risk of your own life.'

"And it came to pass that Esther found within herself the courage to go to the king and she said unto him, 'Oh, gracious majesty, forgive me for entering your chamber uninvited. But it has become known to me that my people are in great peril; that an evil man, named Haman, is planning to destroy them. I beseech you to spare my people.'

"And it came to pass that Esther found favor in the king's eyes and he heeded her plea. And on the very day that Haman had planned to destroy the Jews of Persia he himself was hanged in the middle of the square, by order of the king.

"That is why every year, on the fourteenth day of the Hebrew month of Adar, Jews celebrate the feast of Purim. They send gifts to each other. They tell the story of Esther. And whenever the name of the wicked Haman is mentioned they drown it out with the sound of a wooden noisemaker called the 'grager.'"

"I got it!" Yossele whispered excitedly to Berele. "I got it!"

"Got what?" Berele whispered back.

"The grager."

"I know you have a grager. So have I."

"I mean for the goat," Yossele told him.

"For the goat?" Berele looked puzzled.

Later, during the lunch break, Yossele explained what he meant and Berele agreed it was a good idea. At least it was worth a try.

The next morning Yossele brought his grager with him to the vacant lot. He handed it to Berele and told him to twirl the grager loud and fast as soon as he reached for the goat's front legs, then stop as soon as he started clapping his hands.

It required split-second timing to harmonize the actions. The goat was confused by the rapid changeover from the sound of the grager to the sound of the clapping. And for a while it seemed that the goat would never respond to the grager and that she'd always need the assistance of one of them to rise on her hind legs.

Berele was ready to settle for that, but Yossele wasn't. "If Eliosha could do it, she could, too," he insisted. "I'm not giving up until she does the whole act by herself from start to finish. I know she could do it."

One windy March morning when they least expected it to happen, the goat rose to the sound of the grager and went through the entire act by herself.

It was around this time that Braindel noticed the change in the goat's appearance for which she had long been waiting. The goat looked fuller and heavier. Her bones didn't show as much as before, and she even seemed to have grown a little taller. "Take a look, Yossele," Braindel said, pressing her palm against the goat's ribs. "There's flesh on her bones! It's a miracle! Maybe now she'll start giving a quart a day."

But the goat still continued to give only a half quart of milk a day, not a drop more, not a drop less.

One day, after milking the goat, Braindel looked into the pot and announced, "I've made up my mind. Right after Purim I'm taking her to Reb Beinish the butcher. I think now that she's got some flesh on her Reb Beinish will buy her."

Instantly Yossele's eyes filled with tears. "Please, Mother," he begged, "don't sell her to Reb Beinish."" He bent down and embraced the goat, holding her tight, as though determined never to let go of her. Right now he wished she were skinny again, even skinnier than before. But that miracle, he knew, was not likely to happen. Purim was only three days away and the children were still bringing scraps for the goat.

Braindel saw the pained look on Yossele's face and tried to console him. "I'm doing it with a heavy heart, my son," she said, adding a deep sigh. "I know how attached you've become to

the goat and I wish we could keep her. But I have to do what the rabbi said would have to be done. One doesn't trifle with the rabbi's decision."

Braindel's words were of no comfort to Yossele. All that mattered now was to save the goat from the butcher's cleaver. There were only three days left to do it and he didn't know where to begin. With tears in his eyes he ran to his friend Berele.

The two friends took themselves off to the vacant lot and remained there until it grew dark. By the time they went home they felt much better. They had worked out a plan to save the goat.

On Purim day, Yossele and Berele rose very early to dress up themselves and the goat. They put on their long, loose-fitting patched coats which they had saved in the attic from last Purim, and their three-pointed hamantashen hats they had fashioned from thick cardboard and painted red. Then they rubbed soot on their chins to resemble beards and they were ready.

The goat they dressed up in a three-pointed hamantashen hat which was painted blue. Then they pulled a red ribbon through the ear of a tin cup, tied it around the goat's neck, and the three of them were ready to start out on their rounds.

They went from house to house and everything went just as they had planned it. Yossele twirled the grager and the goat rose on her hind legs; Berele clapped his hands and the goat began to dance. And while the goat danced the two of them sang the Purim song which every child in Betchootch knew by heart:

> *A happy Purim to you all*
> *Let's rejoice in Haman's fall*
> *Haman was an evil man*
> *Wanted all our people dead*
> *But Queen Esther foiled his plan*
> *And he himself was hanged instead*
> *Today is Purim, tomorrow no more*
> *Give us a penny and show us the door*

And when the act was over the tin cup hanging from the goat's neck was clinking with pennies.

But that was only part of the plan. The other part was the children. Yossele and Berele had seen to it that every child in Betchootch knew that the goat was in danger of being sold to the butcher, and that Purim was the last chance to save her.

Dressed in their garish clothes, their faces painted, the children fanned out through the streets of Betchootch and went from house to house as they did on every Purim, to sing the

Purim song and beg for Purim gelt. But this Purim was different from all others. The Purim gelt they asked for was not for themselves but for the goat. "Save the goat! Pennies for the goat!" was the cry they brought to every house they entered.

Later they all stopped off at Braindel's house, on their way home, to empty their pockets. By the time the last of the chil-

dren had come and gone there was a heap of pennies on Braindel's rickety table. Braindel counted them till late into the night and the next morning she took them all to Reb Todres. Ten rubles worth of pennies was a heavy load to carry, but she carried it with a light heart.

Betchootch had always been known for its muddy streets and its wise rabbi, but from that day on it was also known for its dancing Purim goat.

Temple Israel

Minneapolis, Minnesota

In honor of the Bar Mitzvah of
DAVID WIRTSCHAFTER
by
Dr. and Mrs. Jonathan Wirtschafter
June 4, 1983